LET'S LEARN ABOUT
FOOD

WHOLE GRAINS

Samantha Nugent

www.av2books.com

LET'S READ
AV²
BY WEIGL™
ADDED VALUE • AUDIO VISUAL

Go to **www.av2books.com**, and enter this book's unique code.

BOOK CODE

R 5 4 7 8 2 9

AV² by Weigl brings you media enhanced books that support active learning.

AV² provides enriched content that supplements and complements this book. Weigl's AV² books strive to create inspired learning and engage young minds in a total learning experience.

Your AV² Media Enhanced books come alive with...

Audio
Listen to sections of the book read aloud.

Video
Watch informative video clips.

Embedded Weblinks
Gain additional information for research.

Try This!
Complete activities and hands-on experiments.

Key Words
Study vocabulary, and complete a matching word activity.

Quizzes
Test your knowledge.

Slide Show
View images and captions, and prepare a presentation.

... and much, much more!

Published by AV² by Weigl
350 5th Avenue, 59th Floor
New York, NY 10118

Website: www.av2books.com

Library of Congress Control Number: 2015937776

ISBN 978-1-4896-4007-9 (hardcover)
ISBN 978-1-4896-4008-6 (soft cover)
ISBN 978-1-4896-4009-3 (single user eBook)
ISBN 978-1-4896-4010-9 (multi-user eBook)

Printed in the United States of America in Brainerd, Minnesota
1 2 3 4 5 6 7 8 9 0 19 18 17 16 15

062015
160615

Editor: Katie Gillespie   Designer: Mandy Christiansen

Weigl acknowledges Getty Images, iStock, and Corbis as the primary image suppliers for this title.

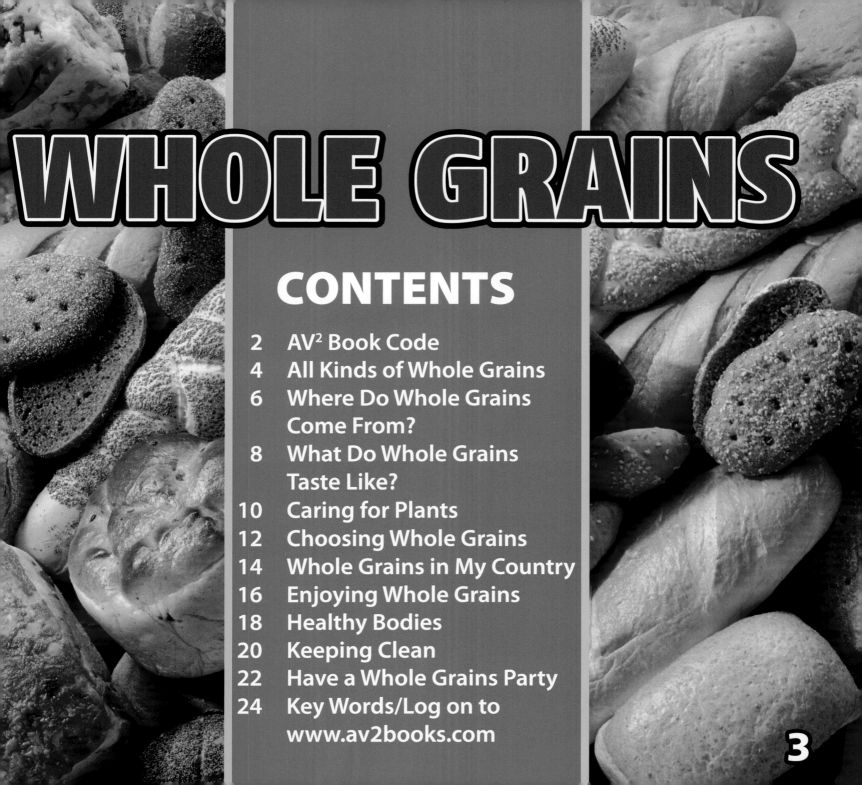

WHOLE GRAINS

CONTENTS

I like to eat whole grain foods. There are many different kinds of whole grains.

Whole grains come from the seeds of plants. Every part of the seed is eaten. Most whole grains come from different kinds of grass plants.

Whole grains grow in big, open fields.

Whole grains often feel soft or chewy. Some whole grains taste sweet. Other whole grains taste like nuts.

I like to eat whole grains at meals and at snack time. Sometimes, I have whole grain foods for dessert.

Farmers give plants plenty of water. This helps the plants to grow and make whole grains.

Plants also need soil, air, and sunshine to grow.

Farmers care for whole grains until they are picked. Trucks take the whole grains away to get them ready to eat.

I help choose my whole grains at the grocery store. Sometimes, I choose whole grain treats from the bakery.

13

Many kinds of whole grains grow in my country. They can be found in many American states.

Corn, barley, and wheat are all grown in America.

Many foods have whole grains in them. Cereal and crackers can both be made with whole grains.

I like to eat foods made with whole grains.

Eating whole grains gives me energy to play.

My body feels healthy when I eat whole grains.

It is important to make sure my whole grains are fresh. The date on the package tells me if my food is still safe to eat.

I wash my hands with soap and warm water before I eat. I sing *Happy Birthday* two times to make sure I have scrubbed long enough.

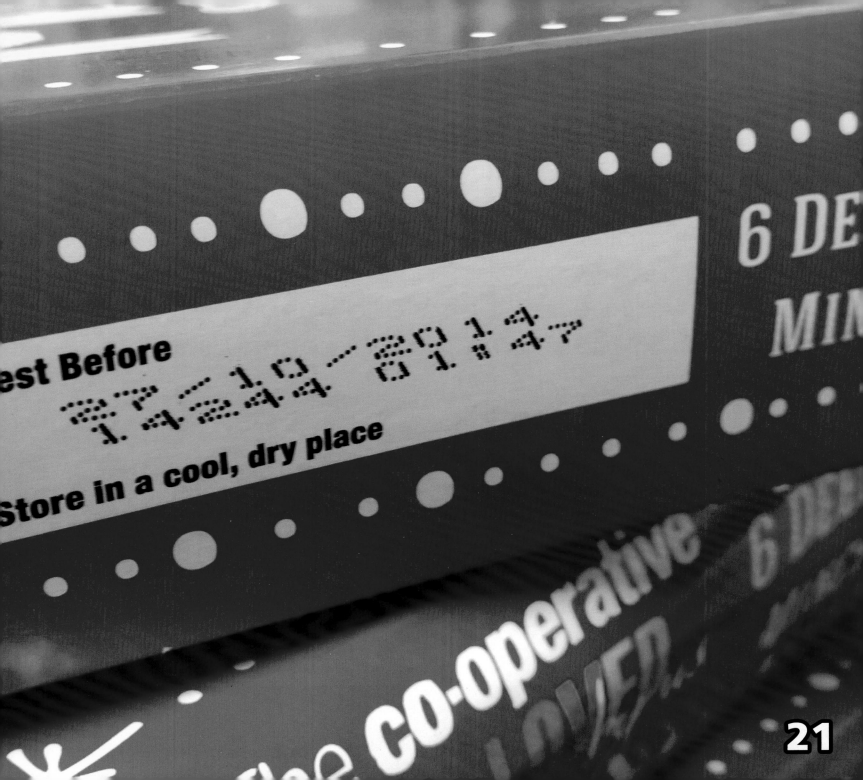

est Before

Store in a cool, dry place

6 DE

MIN

the Co-operative

LOVED

21

How to Make Peanut Butter and Banana Roll-Ups

Whole grains are even better when you share them with your friends and family. Enjoy your peanut butter and banana roll-ups at snack time. This recipe makes enough for four servings.

You will need:

- an adult
- kitchen sink
- 1 dish towel
- 1 butter knife
- 1 cutting board

- 2 whole wheat tortillas
- 2 large bananas
- 1/2 cup (118 milliliters) of peanut butter

Directions

1. Wash your hands with soap and warm water.

2. Run the bananas under cold water and dry them with a clean dish towel.

3. Peel the bananas and set them aside.

4. With an adult's help, use the butter knife to spread peanut butter on one side of each tortilla.

5. Place one banana in the middle of each tortilla and roll it up.

6. Cut the peanut butter and banana roll-ups in half.

7. Share your peanut butter and banana roll-ups with your friends and enjoy!

KEY WORDS

Research has shown that as much as 65 percent of all written material published in English is made up of 300 words. These 300 words cannot be taught using pictures or learned by sounding them out. They must be recognized by sight. This book contains 72 common sight words to help young readers improve their reading fluency and comprehension. This book also teaches young readers several important content words, such as proper nouns. These words are paired with pictures to aid in learning and improve understanding.

Page	Sight Words First Appearance
4	are, different, eat, foods, I, kinds, like, many, of, there, to
7	big, come, every, from, grow, in, is, most, open, part, plants, the
8	and, at, for, have, often, or, other, some, sometimes, time
11	air, also, give, helps, make, need, this, water
12	away, get, my, take, them, they, until
15	all, American, be, can, country, found, states
16	both, made, with
19	me, play, when
20	before, enough, hands, if, important, it, long, on, still, tells, two

Page	Content Words First Appearance
4	whole grains
7	fields, seeds
8	dessert, meals, nuts
11	farmers, soil, sunshine
12	bakery, grocery store, treats, trucks
15	barley, corn, wheat
16	cereal, crackers
19	energy
20	*Happy Birthday*, package, soap

Check out www.av2books.com for activities, videos, audio clips, and more!

1 **Go to www.av2books.com.**

2 **Enter book code.** R 5 4 7 8 2 9

3 **Fuel your imagination online!**

www.av2books.com